LION   HIPPOPOTAMUS   RHINOCEROS   SHOEBILL   BONGO   KIDOGO'S MAMA

LEOPARD

KIDOGO

For Noel, my own Kidogo

Note: The word *kidogo* means *little* in Kiswahili. It is pronounced kee-DOE-go.
Kidogo kidogo means *little by little.*

Copyright © 2005 by Anik Scannell McGrory. All rights reserved.

No part of this book may be used or reproduced in any manner whatsoever without written permission
from the publisher except in the case of brief quotations embodied in critical articles or reviews.

Typeset in TL Pierre Bonnard and Cooper Old Style Light.

The art was created with pencil and watercolor.

Designed by Marikka Tamura.

Published by Bloomsbury Publishing, New York and London. Distributed to the trade by Holtzbrinck Publishers

Library of Congress Cataloging-in-Publication Data

McGrory, Anik.

Kidogo / Anik McGrory—1st U.S. ed.

p. cm.

Summary: Sure that he is the smallest creature on earth, a young elephant leaves home and journeys
over woodlands, rivers, and plains searching for someone even smaller than he is.

ISBN-10: 1-58234-974-6

ISBN-13: 978-1-58234-974-9

[1. Size—Fiction. 2. Size perception—Fiction. 3. Elephants—Fiction. 4. Animals—Fiction.] I. Title.

PZ7.M173Ki 2005   [E]—dc22   2004054729

First U.S. Edition 2005. Printed in Singapore

1 3 5 7 9 10 8 6 4 2

Bloomsbury Publishing Children's Books U.S.A., 175 Fifth Avenue, New York, NY 10010

All papers used by Bloomsbury Publishing are natural, recyclable products made from wood grown in well-managed
forests. The manufacturing processes conform to the environmental regulations of the country of origin.

KIDOGO

ANIK McGRORY

BLOOMSBURY
CHILDREN'S
BOOKS

Kidogo lived in a world that was vast.
He walked under a mountain bigger than the clouds.

He played on endless fields of rippling gold.

And he slept through nights that
were deeper than his dreams.

He was very small . . . for an elephant.

His aunties helped
him reach tender
acacia leaves.

His cousins helped him cross
the flooding river.

His mama helped him with his dust bath,
although he wasn't sure he needed one.

But Kidogo didn't want help.
He didn't want to be the smallest.
So he went off to find someone in the world
who was just as small as he.

He looked in the woodlands.

He looked in the flooding river.

He looked on the plains.

He looked until he knew it was true…

...he was the smallest animal in all the world.

He stopped, lost and alone,
with no place left to look.

He sat and decided.

He wouldn't need anyone else—
big or small.

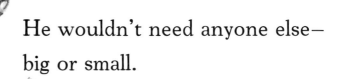

He would find his own
acacia leaves.

He would cross the river by himself.

He would make his own dust bath.
But as the dust fell around him,
there was a tickling and an itching on
his ears and tail and legs and nose.

He swiped and rolled

and brushed

and blew…

…until, finally, the itching stopped.
And there, as he looked down,
was an animal smaller than
he had ever imagined.
Soon he was
surrounded by
tiny animals.

He helped them reach tender acacia leaves.

He helped them cross a flooding river.

He helped them with a dust bath,
although they weren't sure they needed one.

He followed the insects on a march down
the riverbank, through the woodlands,
across the plains, and back to his very own home.

Kidogo saw the insects and the mountains,
little and big. There were his cousins,
his aunties, and his mama.

And Kidogo knew he wasn't too small after all.

He was just right...for a little elephant.

KIDOGO   BUTTERFLY   HORNBILL   JACKAL   VERVET MONKEY   DIK-DIK

ANT   TERMITE   HYRAX   ELEPHANT SHREW   HOOPOE